# CHRISTMAS HORROR

## VOL. 2

DARK REGIONS PRESS, LLC
—2017—

# CHRISTMAS HORROR

## VOL. 2

# CHRISTMAS AT THE PATTERSONS

*Elizabeth Massie*

Donna Wilson didn't always hate Christmas, but she did now. Oh, did she ever. She detested the noise (otherwise known as "Christmas music"), the garish store decorations, the pre-stuffed plastic mesh stockings on sale for pets and kids alike, the chocolate candies dressed up in green and red foil, the artificial Christmas trees, the screamingly cheerful holiday commercials on the radio, and worst of all, the holiday party she and her husband were expected to attend each year at the home of Jeff's boss, Richard Patterson.

The town of Spring Hill was small—population hovering around 9,000—but the

Patterson Empire was big and nearly complete. Richard Patterson owned the hardware store, the grocery store, the weekly newspaper (appropriately renamed the *Patterson News-Register* when he and his wife had moved to town and had taken over thirteen years earlier), the jewelry store, the old-fashioned radio station WRBP, the shoe repair, the Spring Hill Theater, the appliance store, the Maple Leaf Diner, and the Ford dealership. Nearly everyone in town worked for Richard Patterson and nearly everyone in town hated him, though it was a silent hatred, the kind that shown in people's faces when they met one another in the grocery store or passed each other in their Ford vehicles. The citizens needed work. They needed groceries and shoe repairs and, when they had a few bucks in their pockets, they needed to get away to see a movie. And so they endured. They tolerated. Even as Richard Patterson fired some employees and ran others out of town, those who remained kept their hatred sealed up and locked down.

Under the direction of Richard and his crisp scarecrow wife, Bridgett, Christmas in Spring Hill began in late August. Christmas music dominated the airways of WRBP. Stores threw up shiny silver garlands and strings of ornaments and began their "SHOP NOW!" holiday promotions. The telephone and light poles at the intersection of Main and Oak were wrapped in red and white plastic to imitate candy canes. In October, Halloween was a pale shadow of its former self, relegated to the back seat of the Christmas festivities such as nonstop showings of the 1960s television standards, *Frosty the Snowman and Rudoph the Red-Nosed Reindeer* at the Spring Hill Cinema.

The Saturday after Thanksgiving, the Pattersons held an open house at their huge, terrifyingly ornate house on the hill at the edge of town, and attendance was mandatory. Richard and Bridgett decked the halls with every form of Christmas nonsense they could get their hands on. At a distance, the Patterson house looked like a fireball on a hillside or an alien ship come down to Earth, ready to consume all living things within reach.

Donna was one of the few citizens who did not owe her soul to the Pattersons. She had a business selling handmade necklaces and earrings online. It was the one peaceful thing in her life: manipulating thin wires, tiny chains, and hemp strings, then adding glass, shell, and wooden beads of all sizes, shapes, and colors. Her mother, dead now many years, had been a talented crafter herself as well as a soft-spoken yet protective woman with an uncanny ability to drive dogs out of their flower garden with a snap of her fingers and keep bullies away from Donna with a flick of her hand. (Once, when Donna was five, she had laughed and asked Mam if she was a witch or a magic fairy, and Mam only hugged her and said, "I love you, Sweetie.") Donna missed her mother greatly, the comfort and security she had radiated. Yet while Donna had never been the pillar of confidence Mam had been, she had at least inherited Mam's talent with jewelry. The unique pieces she fashioned brought in enough money to keep food in the kitchen for herself and Jeff, who worked at the hardware store and sometimes sneaked materials and tools home to keep their deteriorating doublewide from falling apart.

The night of the Christmas party, Jeff and Donna put on their best outfits. Jeff donned his gray slacks and black jacket. Donna dressed in her black skirt and pale blue blouse, and then opened her jewelry box and took out Mam's favorite necklace, made of tiny shells, dried seeds, and polished little bones. Donna had never worn it before. She'd kept it as a treasure, meant to admire but not use. She turned it over in her hands, remembering how it looked on Mam, how simple and pretty. *I miss you so much*, she thought. On impulse, she clasped it around her neck and grabbed her coat.

Jeff and Donna drove across town and up the winding driveway to the fireball on the hillside. Life-sized mechanical snowmen, reindeer and elves, lined up along the driveway, greeted their arrival, bowing and grinding with shuddering movements, mouths snapping open and closed as if singing Christmas songs. A huge, inflatable snow globe sat beside the indicated parking area, and blazing Tiki torches, tied with red ribbons, lined the sidewalk leading to the front door.

Bridgett Patterson was dressed in a flowing green velvet tunic and wide-leg slacks, star-shaped earrings, jewel-encrusted heeled Gucci sandals, and pink lipstick that sparkled. She greeted guests in the foyer, making kissy lips, tossing her blonde hair, and talking about this-and-that-and-mish-and-mash. Richard stood on the third step in the wide candle-lit foyer, surveying his domain, and then ordered all the men to follow him down the hall to see his "man cave and trophy room" which supposedly held new and even more impressive memorabilia gathered since last December. This left all the women at the mercy of Bridgett, who gathered them in the parlor to tell them the history of each and every Christmas ornament on her eight-foot-tall Frasier fir from Finland.

"Oh, Mrs. Patterson, you have such style and grace!" cooed one of the townswomen, who had hopes that she would be promoted to head saleswoman at the appliance store.

"Yes, it's all so pretty!" crooned another woman who had been without work for months and hoped to get hired at the movie theater.

"You and your husband make Christmas so special!" said another feminine voice, someone who might be hoping Bridgett would float her a loan for next month's mortgage. Donna wasn't paying close attention to the mindless conversation. She stared past the tree to a shadow on the wall, dreading the next four tedious hours, becoming increasingly aware of the fact that the bra she'd chosen to wear was just a little bit too tight, and remembering how Mam never put up with pompous nonsense from anyone.

"And now!" said Bridgett after what might have been an hour, "let's enjoy some tasty holiday treats!"

Bridgett clutched her wine glass in her manicured fingers and tapped her way from the parlor into the grand dining room, where she encouraged her guests to try all the holiday treats spread out silver platters. "I made them all myself, you know. Now, eat up!"

Donna didn't need to be told who'd made the snacks. They tasted like crap. Raisin-tapioca scones with jalapeño glaze. Apricot tarts encrusted with Parmesan cheese. Various hand-rolled dark chocolates filled with crushed garlic, tomato paste, and bacon bits (which Bridgett called "Yuletide Yums.") The women held glass plates and pretended to enjoy the spread. Some choked the offerings down with pained smiles. Others hid bits inside their cloth napkins, waiting for the chance to excuse themselves to the restroom in order to flush the bits away. Bridgett watched them like hawks, sipping her wine, playing with her hair.

"Let's go to the library," said Bridgett after enough of the treats were gone from their platters. "I've prepared a Christmas reading to share with you! The men will be joining us in a little while."

The library was decorated with enough velvet ribbons and pine boughs to choke a one-horse open sleigh. A fire popped in the fireplace.

"Sit down, sit down, everyone!" ordered Bridgett. She lit a Marlboro and it hung from her lower lip as if it had been stapled there. "I've written a poem to share. Now get comfy. I know you'll love this."

The women sat obediently. Donna eased down on the arm of a sofa, fingering her mother's necklace. Mam would have had words with Bridget by now, would have told her to cut it out and quit acting like the Queen of Sheba. Or the queen of Christmas. *Mam had a way with irritating people. If they didn't listen to her she would dismiss them with a wave of her hand and they would go away. Like the dogs in the garden. Like the bully children.*

Donna glanced at the door for a chance to

slip out and make a beeline for the car. Surely Bridgett would look away at some point. Surely she would notice one less guest in the library.

*I hate Christmas.*

"Oh, fair Tannenbaum!" screeched Bridgett around her cigarette. "Empress of trees! Pretty are you, in a cold breezy breeze. Waving and weaving, hello, you say! I'm a Tannenbaum, happy and gay."

The women in the library clutched their knees and forced themselves to smile.

"Oh, fair Tannenbaum, green prickly sticks, you are not ugly like poor ragged hicks."

Donna let out a silent breath. *Look at the window, Bridgett. Just for a moment. That's all I need so I can slip away without you seeing me.*

"Oh, fair Tannenbaum! In silver and gold! Aren't you glad to Pattersons you have been sold?"

*Look at the window, Bridgett. Over there!*

Bridgett sucked hard on the cigarette and it stood out for a moment like a skinny white dick before flopping down again. "Oh, happy Tannenbaum, in your expensive five-hundred-dollar stand. Here at the Pattersons you look quite grand."

*Look at the fucking window, Bridget!*

"Oh, sweet Tannenbaum! Shimmery-shine! Aren't you so glad to say you are mine?"

Donna let out an audible, "Ugh."

All faces swiveled toward hers. The guests looked horrified. Bridget stared, enraged.

"What … was that?" she demanded.

"Phlegm," said Donna. She faked a little cough. "I'm sorry. I was … was trying not to cough and interrupt your lovely reading."

Bridget pursed her pink lips and the cigarette jiggled. She took several steps toward Donna. Her eyes glinted like embers on the hearth. "Who are you, anyway?"

"I'm Donna Wilson. Jeff's wife."

Bridget sniffed. "And who, you irritating little mouse, is Jeff?"

"Jeff Wilson. He works at the hardware store."

"Does he know his wife is rude?"

"I … I wasn't being rude."

Bridgett's lip curled. "Seems to me you hate Christmas, Donna Wilson."

"I don't hate Christmas." *Oh, I do hate Christmas! I do, thanks to you and your self-centered husband!*

"And what have we here?" Bridget reached out for Mam's necklace. "What is that nasty thing?" A brief, orange spark flared on Bridgett's fingertip then vanished.

Donna jumped stepped back before the woman could touch her.

"What kind of jewelry is that?" sneered Bridgett. "Shells? Seeds? Bones? Are you kidding me?"

*I didn't see Bridgett's finger spark! I'm just nervous. My mind's playing tricks.*

"Ladies," laughed Bridgett, "do you see what Donna thought was appropriate to wear around her neck to my Christmas gala? Some kind of trash she picked up on the ground somewhere."

The ladies glanced at each other and nodded. One muttered, "No, not appropriate at all, Ms. Patterson." Another, "No, that's just not right."

Then Bridgett clapped her hands. *Another tiny flash. Another spark?* She smiled broadly, revealing her perfectly straight (*sharp?*) teeth. "Oh, let's let bygones be bygones, shall we? What's a cough and some disgusting garbage stung together in the greater scheme of things? It's Christmas time!"

*No, it's not! It's November, you pompous bitch!*

"I say we toast the season with some sherry! Would you ladies like to join me in a delicious sherry?"

The ladies said yes. Donna felt her own head go up and down slightly.

"Fine, then; follow me!"

Like goslings after a goose, the ladies trailed Bridgett from the library down the main corridor to a more narrow hallway and then up a short flight of stairs and into Bridgett's "lady cave," a smaller room decked out with ancient artworks and poshly puffed pillows, and, of course, several blinking Christmas trees. Bridgett opened an ebony cabinet, revealing crystal glassware and tall bottles filled with amber liquid. "Voila!" As the ladies glanced about at the room and at one another, Bridgett poured liquid into the glasses and passed them around. Then she held her glass aloft.

"Here is to Christmas and to all the fun it brings!"

*I hate sherry. I hate this party!*

"Let's drink to it all!"

*Mam, I wish you were here. There was nothing and no one you couldn't deal with!*

Bridgett downed her drink. The other ladies

drank, too. Donna hesitated, thinking at least it was just a small amount, swallowed hers in a single gulp. *There. Done. And this evening can't be over too soon.*

Then the world began to grow fuzzy.

"Let me tell you about the ornaments on these trees," said Bridgett, her voice growing distant.

Fuzzy and dizzy…

"This one," said Bridgett from far, far away, "cost the most. We got it in Italy …"

… fuzzy and dizzy then dark.

A long, deep darkness.

Total darkness.

Donna's head pounded and her shoulder ached. Her eyes fluttered then opened. She was lying on a sticky vinyl sofa in a shadowy room lit by a single candle on an end table. This was certainly not the "lady cave" nor the library, grand dining room, nor parlor. The place smelled of mildew, feces, and sulfur.

"Party's over, Donna."

Donna forced herself to sit up. *Oww … I hurt!*

"Party's over and everyone gone home, even your precious Jeff." It was Bridgett, somewhere in the shadows. "I told him you confessed to me how you were sick and tired of him, had a lover elsewhere, and were running off, leaving Spring Hill forever."

"What? No. He … he would never believe that."

"Oh, Donna, he would. And he did. So here you are, in my cellar. My little holiday workshop."

"You *drugged* me?"

"You're so slow, aren't you Donna? Did you really think you could say 'ugh' in front of me and my guests? You think you could insult me like that?"

"You drugged me?"

"What do you think?" asked Bridgett, moving out of the shadows to the foot of the sofa. Her arms were crossed. She was still dressed in her green velvet and snowflake earrings, but her hair was less coiffed, a bit tangled, her pink lipstick smeared. She lit a Marlboro and stuck it into her mouth. "That was just the beginning. I don't put up with people like you."

Donna rubbed her shoulder. She must have hit the floor hard.

"The other ladies were sorry to see how poorly

you hold your liquor. 'Oh, poor Donna Wilson,' they said. 'How sad to be such a lush,' they said. 'All wobbly on her feet, and passing out! What a pity,' they said. I promised to let you sleep it off and we moved back to the parlor." Bridgett sat down next to Donna and lit a Marlboro. Donna drew up against the sofa's arm. "Did you like my lawn ornaments?"

"What?"

"Are you as stupid as you look? Of course you are. Lawn ornaments. Or-na-ments."

*Those hideous mechanical monsters along the driveway?* "You mean the snowmen? The reindeer and elves? In front of the house?"

Bridgett blew smoke in Donna's face and Donna coughed. "Yes, idiot," said Bridgett. Did you like them?"

*Mam, help me! What do I do?*

"Well? Answer me? Do you like them?"

"They suck."

Bridgett's eyes widened, whites showing like train lights in a tunnel, barreling forward. "Oh, my. I'm sorry to hear that."

Donna drew herself up and clenched her fists. "I have to go home. I'm going home." *That sounds brave. Brave is good.*

"You're going nowhere, Donna. You're staying here. And you'll make such a lovely Mrs. Santa. Well, not lovely. You are far from lovely. You and that cheap blue blouse. That trashy-ass necklace." Bridgett reached out again. The orange spark was clear this time, and it crackled loudly. Donna jumped to her feet, her head swimming.

"Who are you?" she managed.

Bridgett shrugged, sucked on the Marlboro then exhaled smoke from her nose. No, not smoke. Flames. Tiny flames. "Oh," she said. "I'm me. Just Bridgett Patterson. The woman who gets what she wants when she wants it how she wants it. Nobody denies me. Nobody challenges me."

"You're a witch."

"I don't know, Donna. Maybe. Maybe not. I'm just me. I'm what I want and I get what I want." Bridgett stood and wandered back into the shadows. Donna glanced around, hoping to spot the stairs somewhere in that dark hellhole. Her eyes were still not adjusted and she saw nothing but the shadows, the flickering candle.

Then the overhead light flashed on, brilliant, excruciating. Donna shut her eyes and groaned.

"Oh, quit being such a baby," said Bridgett. "I just want to show you my newest Christmas decoration. Look over here."

Donna slowly opened her eyes. She scanned the room for the steps and saw none, only a closed door. She was in a back cellar room, nowhere near an easy escape. Her heart banged against her ribs; cold sweat stung her arms.

"I said look over here!"

Donna looked.

Standing beside the cinderblock wall, eyes bright with tears, was a life-sized mechanical Santa, stuffed and ruffed and dressed in red and white with shiny black leather boots. His arms made grinding sounds as they opened wide then folded tight across his enormous belly. His head tipped back and forth slowly as his mouth, hinged like that of a ventriloquist's dummy, mimed a silent "ho ho ho."

A silent scream.

"Do you remember Martin Cooper?"

*Martin Cooper. He worked at the grocery store. Big guy. Word was the Pattersons ran him out of town a couple weeks ago.*

"I turned him into the perfect Santa, don't you think? He's next to go out on the front lawn."

"Martin?"

"That's what I said. Oh, but you are so slow. And Martin … I mean Santa … needs a wife. A Mrs. Claus. That's where you come in." Bridgett clapped her hands. Huge sparks leapt from her fingertips, filling the air with an acrid, electric smell. "I love Christmas. Christmas is mine, all mine. Festive and fun!" She giggled and walked toward Donna. Donna backed up. "Now just hold still and it'll be easier. That's what I told Richard right before I changed him, you know. He was such a delicious dork. Such a handsome little moron, my Richard. But now look at him. You'd never know he wasn't real, would you? He does what I say, and because of me, we own Spring Hill and all of you little people."

Donna touched Mam's necklace. It felt strangely warm.

*Mam wore this every day.*

*She would snap her fingers or wave her hand and the dogs and bullies would run away. Fly away.*

*Or did I just imagine it?*

Donna glanced at the door.

"Seriously, Donna? The door's locked, you

must know that. You aren't going anywhere, except out on my front lawn along the driveway as Mrs. Claus." Bridgett took a drag on the cigarette and shot two columns of fire from her nostrils.

*Mam took a long time choosing the seeds, the shells, the bones. The perfect combination. Crafted with precision, with her rare and special talent.*

"Now," said Bridgett. "A woman for Santa! A friend! A wife!" She raised her hands and flames trailed like hellish ribbons. "Be still now and it won't hurt too much."

Donna raised her hand at the same moment and flicked her wrist. Bridgett was knocked backward toward the weeping, creaking mechanical Santa and hit the floor.

*Yes!*

Bridgett scrambled to her feet and stumbled forward two steps. Her hair was mussed, her composure shot. "What was that? Who are you?" she screeched.

"Maybe I'm the ghost of all the Christmases you fucked up." Donna flicked her hand a second time, harder, sending Bridgett backward again, even closer to Santa this time.

"You can't do that!" wailed Bridgett. Flames

of rage shot from her nose and mouth and singed the sleeves of her velvet pantsuit. "No! I will have what I want when I want as I want!" She clawed her way up and charged Donna.

"Get lost, you dog!" said Donna, and she flicked her hand once more. Bridgett was flung fully across the room and slammed into Santa, whose open arms closed around her and snapped her neck. Bridgett's eyes popped; her knees buckled. The flames from her mouth and nose dissolved into trails of smoke. The cigarette in her hand dropped, bounced off the toe of one Gucci sandal, and rolled away.

"You might love Christmas," said Donna. "But it looks like Christmas hates you."

Santa began to melt back into Martin Cooper, the rigid machinery softening, drooping, leaving a heavyset man in a Santa costume, panting, staring in wonder at Donna and then at the dead woman on the floor.

"Come on, Martin," said Donna. "This place stinks."

Outside on the lawn, the ornaments were coming back to life. Missing citizens morphed from mechanical to human. They slumped to the frosty ground, rubbing necks, coughing, crying. They watched Donna as she walked past them, nodding sympathetically and whispering, "Merry Christmas."

At the base of the driveway, Donna turned to gaze back up at the house on the hill and the Tiki torches blazing by the front porch. She waved her hand and the torches flew up and crashed through the first-floor windows. In a matter of moments, flames were dancing deep inside the house.

Donna drew her coat around her and walked home, smiling at the holiday lights in town, grinning up at the first white flakes of snow that drifted down like ash from a burning mansion.

# LITTLE WARRIORS

*Gene O'Neill*

## PROLOGUE

On Mt. George, near the old Monticello-to -Napa wagon trail, December 2015—

*Around midnight, near the still-standing redwood shed, which had served in the past as a halfway horse-changing station for the wagons back-hauling quicksilver to Napa from Monticello, hundreds of greenish-blue dots coalesced into a luminescent existence. For a moment, the amorphous figure, about the size of a large hummingbird, hovered as if gaining its bearings; then, just an iridescent blur, it zoomed three-quarters of the way up Mt. George and quickly disappeared beneath the shadowed decking extending across the western face of the darkened adobe home.*

**1**

The Arthur brothers, Jake and Little Anthony —his nickname ironic because he stood six foot three, only half an inch shorter than his older brother—were waiting for their sidekick, Wilton Smith, Jr. Wilton, better known on the Oakland streets as Repeat, was shopping to find a proper-fitting set of snowshoes for his childlike feet. The recently paroled trio had already been to two other places, including REI in Berkeley, with no luck, and the brothers were now waiting impatiently outside Snowdrift Ski Shop in Moraga, standing next to their '91 Escort station wagon—a heavily decorated survivor of the Oakland parking wars.

The ex-cons had made recent plans for a series of potential big-score burglaries, but they'd all need snowshoes for the robberies. They planned on taking advantage of the early snow flurries right after Thanksgiving and the subsequent heavier snowfalls in December that had recently closed down State Highway 89 around the southwestern edge of Lake Tahoe.

"Lots of wealthy hotshots from the Bay Area have cabins isolated by the snow up there now," Little Anthony had explained earlier in the day—he was the leader of the group. "We'll borrow Big Mack's four-wheel-drive Dodge Ram pickup, break into a couple of the boarded-up smaller cabins just off eighty-nine at night … and then the next day we'll hit some of the bigger chalets nearer Squaw Valley and the other ski lifts. If the rich people are even up there for Christmas vacation, you can bet your sweet asses they'll be off skiing during the day, leaving behind all their expensive Christmas presents still wrapped."

The smaller man appeared suddenly, running out of the front doors of Snowdrift, quickly approaching the parked junker and proudly waving his new pair of children's snowshoes overhead like two tennis rackets, grinning excitedly, but stalling out when he tried to explain. "L-L-L-L—"

Jake put his arm around his hyper cohort's shoulders, hugged him tightly, and quietly said, "Okay, bro. Now ya just take a deep breath in and out … and calm the fook down, ya unnerstan what I'm sayin?"

Repeat nodded, sucked in a long breath, let it out slowly, and then tried to talk again, but could only manage, "G-G-G—" He stomped his foot violently on the asphalt, which jarred loose an explosive "Got 'em, fellas!"

To a casual stranger, his stunted stature, pronounced stammer, and bizarre facial tics made Repeat appear physically/intellectually challenged. But even though the little ex-con was gullible, naïve, and childlike at times, he was also a certified badass in a tight spot. He'd once saved Little Anthony from being slashed on the main yard at San Quentin by charging and head-butting a Black Guerilla, knocking the prison gang member flat on his back, and then disarming the semi-conscious man of his weapon—a piece of safety razor melted into the head of a plastic toothbrush handle. Fortunately for them, all three were transferred to the CCC near Susanville, a minimum-security prison camp in Northern California, a few days after the hushed-up incident without having to face Department of Corrections discipline or, more importantly, deadly BG retaliation. The Arthur brothers never forgot Repeat's brave action.

**2**

Tanner McKinney waited anxiously at the foot
of the Southwest Airline Terminal escalator to
the baggage claim on the street level at Oakland
Airport for Sally and the twins to appear. Their
flight from San Diego had been delayed over
an hour and a half by regional thunderstorms,
which seldom, if ever, occurred in San Diego in
December. He was anxious because Sally and
the kids had been living with her older sister,
Lilly, in Carlsbad during a trial separation. He
hadn't seen any of them for over three months.
Now, he was hopeful that the family could
finally be reunited permanently. He was going
to do his best to make it happen, and it sounded
like Sally was more than a bit willing to give
it a sincere try. She'd agreed on spending the
kids' *entire* Christmas vacation at his family's
adobe cabin isolated on the western slope of
Mt. George—the highest point on the eastern
side of Napa Valley. He was relieved because his
earliest memories as a youngster included the
yearly McKinney clan tradition of gathering
for Christmas at the adobe on Mt. George.
In recent years, the extended family had been

shrinking in numbers, partly due to some of the younger members having moved away from the Bay Area, but also to an increasing number of older family members passing. Now, it was just Tanner, his immediate family, and his brother, Mike. He was thankful they would be reunited and continue the thirty-plus years of McKinney Christmas tradition atop Mt. George.

Tanner was busy scanning the faces of descending passengers, afraid he'd miss his family in the tightly packed departure crowd. Sally was petite, the twins mirroring her tiny stature. As his family appeared in view, his favorite Christmas Carol, "The Little Drummer Boy," began playing throughout the terminal—*Brrrum, brum, brum, brum ...*

"Hey, Pops," Sean shouted, waving as he led the family onto the down escalator. The fourteen-year-old wasn't usually so publicly demonstrative. But Sinead, his twin sister, was right behind him, characteristically jumping up and down, waving over peoples' heads. Sally brought up the rear, looking down at him and smiling broadly.

Because of the long hours at his computer day job at Cisco Systems and then writing half the night and every weekend during the year past, Sally had complained of him being inattentive to the family. It was true; he had not been there for any of them. But he'd ignored all three even more during the last six months, because he thought he was on the verge of breaking into the big time with one of his thriller novels. He'd secured a good NYC agent who had agreed with that assessment of *The New Plague*, but had forwarded along thirty or so single-spaced pages of complicated suggested edits and revisions. Then, in the middle of those revisions at the end of last August, Sally had shocked him: taking matters into her own hands, abruptly packing up some necessities, and leaving their apartment in San Francisco with the kids for Carlsbad.

Negotiations over the phone the last week or so had been promising. Watching them descend on the escalator, Tanner waved back, his spirits lifting and taking the edge off his nervousness.

On the ground floor, they all hugged, Sally kissing him on the lips—just a trace firmer than an old garden-variety-greeting peck. And she whispered, "Missed you, Mr. T." The family huddled up and chatted about the flight delay while they waited five minutes to pick up their luggage. Then, bags in hand, Tanner led them to the parked Lexus SUV with the tiny Christmas tree riding in the rack on top. As was tradition, the family would decorate a tree at the adobe.

Even at 4 o'clock, the Friday night commuter traffic from the Oakland Airport west on I-880 and then north on I-80 was gridlocked, much worse than usual. With school out for Christmas vacation, perhaps many were already heading up to the ski resorts at Stateline and Lake Tahoe—there had been flurries of snowstorms right after Thanksgiving up until the present. The stop-and-go progress on the freeway gave the family a chance to relax, everyone perhaps feeling a bit stiff after the almost-four-month separation. The constant stream of Christmas music on the radio also helped put everyone in a relaxed, joyful mood.

Tanner asked the kids about their new school. The twins had been good students in San Francisco and were presently enrolled in the eighth grade at the famed Children's School near UC San Diego in La Jolla.

"Going great, Pops," Sean said. "Our modern

Christmas play was really fun and turned out well. Good audience reactions. I helped write it and was a kinda hippie guru wearing a tie-dyed outfit. Sinead starred as San Diego Lou, a country-western guitar player, who sang, "Crazy" and "Mamas Don't Let Your Babies Grow Up To Be—"

"Sean, you were supposed to let *me* tell Dad!" Sinead interrupted.

Her brother shrugged and said, "Oh, *sorry*," his dismissive tone indicating he wasn't the least bit concerned about his sister's disappointed outburst.

Both rambled on about the new school, their teachers, and especially a bunch of new friends. Sounded to Tanner like they both had adjusted exceptionally well for teenagers being disrupted from their routine on short notice, and then leaving behind all their old friends at University Middle School in San Francisco.

"Dad, did Uncle Mike get off work early in Sacramento, and will he be here tonight at the cabin?" Sinead asked. The twins were tight with his much-younger single brother. Mike had bonded with them when they were ten years old, teaching them basic and advanced archery skills and taking them to many junior competitions around the country. Recently, he'd told Tanner and Sally that he thought the twins had the ability to compete internationally, perhaps even a chance of making the Olympic archery team and going to Rio de Janeiro next year, but probably a lock for making the team for Tokyo in 2020.

Tanner smiled inwardly. His brother was a lifelong skilled bowhunter, and had promised to take the twins deer and boar hunting when they turned sixteen. A year ago, Mike had set up a tough training schedule, the pair practicing religiously three days a week at the South City Archers' Club. On weekends, whenever possible, they would go up and shoot at least one day at Mike's private archery club near Rocklin—Billy Tell's Red Apple Range.

"Not tonight, but Uncle Mike will be up late tomorrow evening or early Sunday morning," Tanner said.

"He's planning on staying on for Christmas Eve, right?" Sally asked.

Tanner nodded. "He said he wouldn't miss it, had some special gifts for his *favorite* niece and nephew."

"We're his *only* niece and nephew, Pops," Sean said, chuckling at his uncle's old joke.

The family was fairly relaxed now, enjoying each other's company and the background Christmas music, even though the commuter traffic was still stop-and-go. But eventually it thinned significantly as they crossed over the Carquinez Bridge on I-80 and passed by the eastern turnoff for Benicia on the southern outskirts of Vallejo.

"Looks like it'll be too dark to practice anyhow if we *ever* do get to the cabin this evening," Sinead complained, disappointed resignation obvious in her tone. It was already beginning to turn dusk. They'd both been working on their quick pull, aim and release technique at pop-ups at a San Diego archery club, but they wanted to get down as soon as possible to practice the technique at the new target range their uncle had cleared: a long level spot near the old Monticello-to-Napa historic wagon trail—a pair of stationary targets using the horse shed as a backdrop.

"You guys can go down tomorrow morning, get in some practice before Uncle Mike gets here," Sally suggested. She'd strongly encouraged the small but athletic youngsters' almost obsessive interest in archery, although she was alarmed by Mike's recent offer to take them out bowhunting a year or so from now. That sounded a bit too dangerous to her.

Tanner glanced at the twins in the back seat, smiled, and nodded. "You can show off for Uncle Mike tomorrow night or Sunday morning after he gets here."

At about 7:10, the McKinney family finally pulled into the circular driveway in front of the family place. Then they hauled their luggage into the sprawling adobe. Quickly dropping off their stuff into the three bedrooms, they all met out on the long deck spanning the back of the house and enjoyed the spectacular view, everywhere below them Napa Christmas lights sparkling. After a few minutes, Tanner walked to the southern end of the deck, looked down, and checked out the attached old-fashioned greenhouse. Everything was still apparently intact, including all the multi-paned glass windows. Overhead, the stars were twinkling, and to the south, thirty-five miles away, the red and green lights from San Francisco were shining brightly, as were the lights of St. Helena, away up-valley about ten or eleven miles. As the family enjoyed the sights, the full moon rose over the mountain behind them, bathing the Napa Valley directly below them in silvery, eerie moonlight.

Sinead stared down at the barely visible old wagon trail looping around from northeast to southwest halfway down the mountain, and then said, "Look, you can even make out the two archery targets Uncle Mike set up behind the horse-changing shed."

Tanner nodded and said, "Some of your great-grandfather Harry's ashes are scattered beside that horse shed … just north of that nearby spring." The spring had been capped long ago, and a deep depression left unfilled was hidden by ground cover, including wild blackberries, growing thickly.

"Your gramps personally built that redwood horse shed, right, Pops?" Sean said.

"Yes, just after he built this adobe and great viewing porch." Thinking back for a moment, Tanner laughed. "When I first came up here as a youngster, the old boy had five hummingbird feeders hanging along this decking. He loved and admired the feisty little devils as his *personal* animal totems. Claimed they showed some of our family's Gaelic fighting spirit. In fact, he often called them 'Little Warriors.'" Tanner smiled wryly to himself. Even folks who knew Gramps well would've never guessed the tough old bird's private hobby back then. He'd built the greenhouse attached to the south side of the house to raise rare orchids.

"Harry was indeed an interesting man," Sally said, leading the others back inside the sliding glass doors. She'd never met the family patriarch, who'd died thirty-some years ago, but she'd heard many of the McKinney family legends about his nature and exploits. "After finally retiring at seventy-seven he hiked for a month above 15,000 feet in the Himalayas."

Later that night, they decorated the Christmas tree, brought in and spread out the presents from the car. They'd actually begin their yearly tradition tomorrow night: reading a Christmas story, and opening one present each of the five nights before Christmas Eve. Saturday night, it would be Sinead's turn to read O. Henry's wonderful story, "The Gift of the Magi."

❋

Early Saturday morning Sinead rushed into her mom and dad's master bedroom, her cheeks a rosy red and shouted, "Come quick, outside! You guys aren't going to believe this."

Alarmed, the parents struggled up out of the warm tangle of covers, hurrying into a *freezing* front room in their skimpy nightclothes—the twin had left the front door wide open.

Everywhere outside was totally blanketed in white, including where Sean was standing in the middle of the circular driveway near the storage shed.

It had snowed last night while they all were sleeping.

The adults looked around with disbelief, because it *never* snowed here in the Valley … or anywhere in the Bay Area. But it had last night, and it'd been heavy. The snow was deep enough to almost cover Sean's Converses—

Barefoot, Sally shivered in her thin negligee, and with teeth chattering she said to the family, "Let's all get back inside before we freeze and dress up warmer. Maybe get a cup of hot chocolate down, before we come back out to play in this strange stuff." Of course they didn't have gloves or snow parkas or even hooded winter coats, but they could all wear sweatshirts under their lined raincoats. Sally had fortunately packed them for her and the twins, and had insisted that Tanner bring his along in case. There was occasionally some rain in the valley in December, and especially up here on Mt. George.

### 3

Naturally, Jake, Little Anthony, and Repeat had adjusted their plans as soon as they saw it snowing earlier that morning and heard the Bay Area weather forecasts—a fifty-year snowstorm was predicted to hit later, a possible whiteout at higher elevations by nightfall. They realized they didn't have to drive five or six hours from Oakland up to Tahoe for good isolated burglary targets. Instead, Little Anthony had suggested, "Let's head up to the Napa Valley, lots of rich people with places in the eastern foothills. Me and Jake know that area pretty well."

Repeat grinned and said, "G-G-Good deal."

"Yeah, years ago, when we were jus kids livin in nearby American Canyon, we caddied at the swanky Napa Country Club off Hagen Road," Jake said. "Ha, before they fired our raggedy asses, ya unnerstan."

"W-what for?" Repeat asked.

"The caddy master claimed we were stealin cigarettes, lighters, gum, and change from customers' golf bags," Jake replied and shrugged with a sly grin. "So we kicked the shit out of him, and then gotta hat. We knew the pussy would sic the cops on us if we hung around."

He ended the story right there … and the three cohorts all laughed with

devilish delight.

**4**

It began snowing again before noon, and by mid-afternoon in some places it was almost a foot deep, especially along the south side of the adobe and greenhouse, smaller drifts piling up on the exposed hundred yards or so of the narrow access road before it wound down northeasterly and disappeared into the cover of the thick forest of madrone, oak, and pine trees.

Mike had called just before dinner, and said that he'd heard about the freak snowstorm in the Valley, but he still planned on being up there sometime tomorrow morning. He drove an older Jeep for hunting, which had four-wheel drive and good tires. State Highway 121 up from the Napa Valley floor would probably be plowed clear by then, he'd said, because it was the only access from Napa to Wooden Valley and the town of Winters. And the mile of unplowed private steep road that turned off 121 and climbed up the leeward side of the mountain to the adobe was fairly well protected by the thick forest. So Uncle Mike was confident of making it despite the predicted heavy snowfall later in the evening.

### 5

By dark, the three ex-cons had driven to the eastern Napa Valley foothills, the end of Hagen Road, which actually merged with the non-graded southern end of the historic Monticello-to-Napa wagon trail. In the four-wheel-drive pickup they made it as far as possible along the narrow, rocky trail, parking close to the less-steep southern slope of Mt. George. First they put on their disguises as the three Wise Men—striped bathrobes and towels wrapped on their heads as turbans. If they got stopped by the law on the way up or leaving, they'd claim they were going to a Christmas party. Then they slipped into their snowshoes and backpacks. Repeat was armed with a sawed-off ten-gauge shotgun, and the Arthur brothers both carried Glock 9mm automatics, K-bars, and plastic handcuffs in their backpacks. They began plodding the quarter of a mile along the old wagon trail, then climbed straight up a draw toward lights shining in a place about three-quarters of the way up the mountain. Had to be rich guys living way up there … They finally stopped to catch their breath at the steps leading up to a long porch, took their nylon stocking masks out of their backpacks, and slipped them on.

## 6

After wolfing down a microwave pizza, the family was gathered around the big dining-room table to listen to Sinead read "The Gift of the Magi." She'd neared the end of the ironic story, where the poor young couple are exchanging their wrapped presents. He'd sold his only valuable possession, an antique watch, to buy her a decorated comb for her beautiful hair, and she'd sold her long tresses to buy him a watch fob.

At that moment Sally glanced up ... and sucked in a gasp. Three two-thousand-year-old revenants resembling the Wise Men, supernaturally conjured up by the story, were hovering and looking in the porch window. She finally managed a scream.

The oddly dressed figures, with weirdly distorted features, were sliding the unlocked glass door fully open.

"Hey, hold it, right there!" Tanner shouted, jumping up from the table, hurrying across the dining room, and confronting the intruders, who were all wearing nylon stocking masks disguising their faces.

"S-S-Shut up," the smallest man said, stepping forward and deftly tapping Tanner squarely in the face with the butt of his shotgun.

Tanner retained consciousness but sagged to his knees, cupping his hand to his bloody nose and cut lip. By then the family was upset and badly frightened.

Sally overcame her initial shock, moved over and kneeled at Tanner's side, trying to staunch the bleeding with her apron.

"Okay folks," one of the big men said calmly, but gesturing with an automatic handgun, "no one needs to get hurt like Sir Galahad here, *if* y'all listen carefully and follow orders. Okay?"

The stunned twins remained seated, speechless and looking wide-eyed at the armed spokesman … but finally nodded.

"Anyone armed, or guns stashed here?"

Sally shook her head.

"Good. We need all cell phones on the table *right* now." The twins reached into their hip pockets and complied. Sally said that hers was on the sink in the kitchen.

"Get it," the big man ordered. He pointed his handgun at Tanner, who was still dazed, but able to sit up on the floor where he'd landed. "Galahad, ya got a cell-phone?"

Tanner nodded his head, his nose aching badly but only dribbling slightly now. He dug out his phone, and Sally put it on the table for him.

"Landlines are where?"

"They aren't connected," Sally, who had almost pulled herself together, explained in a voice just a tiny bit higher-pitched than normal. "No one has lived here for years. We're only here for our traditional Christmas vacation." She figured since the intruders were masked the family's lives weren't endangered if they cooperated.

"Okay," the spokesman continued, "all wallets, purses, and jewelry on the table."

After a minute, everyone had complied, Sinead and Sally getting their purses from where they hung near the front door in the hallway.

"You bring any other valuables here into the house ... like money, other jewelry, watches, or expensive Christmas presents, stuff like that?"

Tanner and Sean handed over their watches.

After reluctantly taking off her diamond stud earrings and wedding ring, Sally slowly shook her head. "Nothing else I can think of ... except for the Christmas presents, under the tree in the living room. And they aren't really expensive stuff anyhow—just some video games, books, and kids' clothes. We planned on a week of hiking and quietly celebrating Christmas here on the mountain. Didn't bring any fancy jewelry or anything for dressing up."

"We'll look the presents over later." The leader turned to his two associates.

"Repeat, check out the house. Make sure all phone lines are dead. Jake, check those stairs, see what's down there."

"May I get ice for my husband's nose, give him some aspirin from my purse?" Sally asked. She'd been a RN when they were first married eighteen years ago, and remembered what to do to ease Tanner's immediate pain and facial swelling.

"Sure, lady, get him some aspirin and ice … But remember I'm watching. You're much too pretty to be sporting a bullet hole. Okay?"

She nodded and went to get ice from the kitchen fridge, her purse still on the dining room table.

She was attending Tanner, when the man named Jake came back upstairs and reported. "It's kinda unfinished basement with a pair of beds down there. No doors or windows, the foundation sittin on exposed rock in places. Phone's definitely dead. Saw a big chest against the far wall, but it's empty. Lots of fookin books in a pair of bookcases, mostly paperbacks. Dint

❉ 49 ❉

see nothin of real value, ya unnerstan—"

The small man came hustling back into the dining room, obviously excited.

"C-C-C—" He stomped, broke his stammer and said, "Come see w-what I found accidentally, Lil Anthony."

The brothers herded the family ahead of them, following Repeat into the tiny office off from the master bedroom. He pointed at the floor between the desk and southern wall.

A throw rug was kicked over, and revealed a small floor safe.

Little Anthony forced a thin-lipped grin. "Well now," he said, staring menacingly at Sally, who was looking down at the safe with surprise written on her face. "Nothing else of value here, eh? What's the combination, lady?"

She frowned, and then shook her head. "We've never used it. Don't remember ever noticing it before. Must've been hidden by that throw rug the times we visited in the past."

"How bout it, Galahad?"

"Forgotten it was there," Tanner answered, his stuffed-up voice affected by his injured nose. "It was my grandfather who built the place. He owned the wagon line between Napa and Monticello. But he had his shipping office down in Napa on the river where they off-loaded the wagons onto barges destined for the city. I don't think anything of value was *ever* kept up here...." He paused before adding, "This safe probably hasn't been used or even opened by anyone for maybe ... thirty or more years since he died—"

"C'mon, man, do we look like fucking *idiots*?" Little Anthony snapped angrily. "Ya shitting me? Nobody ever curious about what was in that safe for over thirty years?"

Tanner just shrugged innocently in an apologetic manner.

"Well, maybe we can jog some memories," the leader said, looking at his smaller friend. "Anything else of value on this floor, Repeat?"

The little man shook his head.

"Okay, Jake, let's talk to mama and papa back there at the dining room table," Little Anthony said, his tone more than a hint ominous. Then, gesturing with his handgun, he said, "Repeat, take these two kids down and lock em in the basement for now, while we *discuss* things privately with their folks."

## 7

It was getting cold in the basement. The twins had slept down there several times in the past during larger family gatherings, especially when their Uncle Mike came up.

Tonight, they stripped a blanket from each of the beds, wrapped them around their shoulders; but they were scared wide-awake, afraid almost to breathe, listening intently, and whispering. The voices above were muffled, but most of what was said was still intelligible.

It didn't sound like the thieves believed their parents about not knowing the floor safe combination. The crooks suspected their parents either knew or it had to be written down somewhere here in the adobe, and they wanted it. At first, they just bullied their parents verbally....

But as the night wore on, the twins cringed, huddling and holding each other closer, flinching as the dangerous crooks lost patience and began to get physical, a number of loud slaps echoing through the floor and across the basement. It sounded like they were going to torture their dad in front of their mother.

"Okay, Repeat, get my K-bar out, saw off his little finger—"

"No, please, noooo …"

"That was *Mom*," Sinead whispered, the blankets held tightly around their shoulders.

Sean nodded, but put a finger to his lips.

"We don't know, I swear," their mom added, between loud sobs. "You've cut him for nothing."

It was quiet for a long while, but a decision was finally made.

"Okay, Galahad, let's see if we can jog *your* memory," the leader said, his tone sharp and serious. "Strip off all your clothes *now*, lady. We're gonna play some grab-ass."

The twins held their collective breaths, not really believing the speaker's obvious intent….

*"Enough!"*

That last angry roar was from their dad.

Immediately, there followed the sounds of a major scuffle overhead, loud thumps and things being thrown around or knocked over and then a sudden—

*Bang.*

"Oh, man, you didn't have to shoot him."

"You dirty, evil bastard…" That was their mother shrieking and attacking the shooter.

*Bang.*

"They shot them both?" Sinead whispered, in a stunned, incredulous voice.

With tears in his eyes, and a horror-struck expression, Sean shuddered but placed his forefinger to his lips again. "*Shush.*"

Nothing.

It was dead quiet above them for what seemed like an eternity.

And then an angry exclamation, "Goddammit, Jake! We ain't ever going to get that combination, now," the leader said, obviously upset. "The kids probably doan know shit about it."

In a choked-up voice, Sean whispered to his sister, "They're both definitely *gone.*"

Sinead just sat still on the edge of the bed, looking like a small child suddenly awakened and terrified of drowning in the dark, too shocked to reply, huge tears rolling slowly down her cheeks ... and then, as if grasping onto a lifeline in the dark, she shook herself and thought *Well, they are back together now ... forever.*

"We're going to be next!"

Her brother's sudden dreadful assessment shocked Sinead back to at least partial reality.

"We need to get out of here, *right now*," Sean added.

Sinead glanced around, as if seeing the basement for the first time—no windows, only the one locked door, *no* other way out of this basement that she could see. "How?" she whispered hoarsely.

Both twins remained in place, shocked into inaction by the horrifying murder of their parents.

But at that moment a neon bluish-green apparition appeared in the cellar.

"What is it?" Sean said, a puzzled look on his face.

It seemed like a kind of brightly translucent hummingbird to Sinead, about the size of her fist. It hovered over the chest against the far wall for only a moment, then dropped down behind the chest and disappeared out of sight. After a few seconds, the iridescent figure reappeared and disappeared again, repeating the odd process two more times.

Finally wiping her eyes again with the back of her wrist, Sinead said in a hoarse whisper, "Sean, I think it's some kind of friendly creature and wants us to follow."

Sean nodded as the brightly colored thing disappeared again. He pulled the empty chest away from the wall, revealing the concrete foundation, spanning a rocky outcropping. The figure had disappeared into an upside-down V-like rocky crevice below the foundation that had been hidden by the chest. The opening looked just large enough for them both to crawl through.

The twins, dragging their blankets behind, wiggled through the crevice under the foundation, finding themselves in a small depression under the foot-wide floorboards of the greenhouse. They pushed two of the old floorboards loose and slid them over, exposing a wide space. Then both scrambled up into the greenhouse. They cloaked themselves again in their blankets, even though it felt a bit warmer here. But the air smelled stale. Sean led his sister over to the outside door of the greenhouse and signaled *Wait*. He spit several times on the hinges, which were a bit rusty from years of non-use. Finally, with care, they both quietly leaned in and managed to force the stuck door open just enough to squeeze through.

Outside, the snowing had subsided, but the

temperature had continued to drop.

It had to be below freezing.

"Let's get our bows," Sean whispered, pointing at the storage shed in the center of the turnaround. Glancing back at the house and seeing no one watching out the glass of the front door, the twins made their way quickly to the shed. Their unstrung practice bows were hung on pegs inside the unlocked shed—neither was weighted or balanced like their more expensive competition bows left down in Carlsbad and up at their uncle's place in Sacramento. There were five or six arrows in each of the two hanging quivers, but none with razor-sharp hunting tips; only thimble-like blunt metal practice tips. The practice arrows were better than nothing.

Sean said, "We need to get away, find a sheltered place to hide for three or four hours until dawn, when it will hopefully warm up. We won't make it very far in the dark in this chilling cold, wading through deep snow. Especially if our Converses get wet."

"Let's hide out in the horse shed down on the old wagon trail," Sinead suggested. "Then maybe we can get out to Highway 121 after the sun rises and hitch a ride."

❋

Down at the horse shed, the twins huddled under their two blankets, their feet remarkably dry but frozen numb, both teens much too cold to sleep, the two gunshots continuing to echo frightfully in their memories. They took off their shoes and rubbed some life into each other's feet. Somehow they managed to weather the remaining few hours of night, shivering as much with fear as with the icy chill. They knew the killers would be coming for them soon.

**8**

The three cohorts found the basement empty shortly after shooting the twin's parents. But, knowing the two youngsters couldn't get far in the knee-deep snow during the freezing night, Little Anthony had suggested, "We'll wait until dawn, then track the lil shits' footprints in the snow. We'll catch up to them wearing our snowshoes. Let's get a few hours rest."

As the sun rose over Mt. George, the three easily tracked the twin's footprints down to where the youngsters had left the access road to wade through deep snow to reach the old wagon trail. It had stopped snowing sometime during the night, but was freezing cold.

The killers, who had abandoned their turbans and masks, paused on the wagon trail, Little Anthony pointing down at the old horse shed. "The lil shits are holed up down there. See where their fucking tracks are leading?"

They walked several hundred yards closer, until they were easily within shouting distance. Little Anthony signaled for the trio to stop. Then he yelled, "Come out, you two. We ain't gonna hurt you if you give up. We just wanta ask you a few questions. Then you can go back up the mountain to the warm house, where we left your folks tied up. They're really worried about you."

**9**

The twins had heard the killers coming before the leader shouted out. Sean shook his head emphatically when the man said that they wouldn't be hurt. "They won't let us off this mountain alive, Sinead," he whispered, his lips blue with the cold. "Our folks aren't tied up at the house, they're *gone*. And now we've seen the killers' bare faces through the cracks in the shed wall, and know their first names."

Sinead nodded, trying to stomp feeling into her still chilled feet. She was so tired.

**10**

The luminescent creature appeared again just beyond the blackberry bushes below the capped spring.

Repeat saw it first and shouted, "L-L-Look! It must be Tinkerbell!" Then he began to run awkwardly in his snowshoes toward the hovering translucent apparition.

Suddenly, he disappeared, falling into the capped-spring depression. He didn't come up. The brothers ran to the edge of the hole and looked down.

"*Jesus*," Jake said, careful not to fall in and join his friend, who was not moving, his head twisted slightly to the side, his forehead and face completely covered with blood. He looked up, but the iridescent creature had disappeared. "What the fook was that thing?"

"Who knows," Little Anthony said, pulling his brother back. "Repeat is history, man. Leave his ass."

They stepped back from the pit and glared down at the horse shed.

They both jacked rounds into the chambers of their automatics.

## 11

The frozen, frightened twins watched the accident play out through the wall cracks, the two killers standing still now at the edge of the capped spring, looking frozen, frightened twins watched the accident play out through the wall cracks, the two killers standing still now at the edge of the capped spring, looking mean-spirited and menacing.

Finally, Sean seemed to come to life. He strung his bow and, even with frozen hands, notched an arrow. "Dad said that his Grandpa Harry claimed we came from Gaelic warrior stock, Sinead. We can't just wait here to be shot to death by these two ruthless assholes. It's time for us to stand up and fight back!"

Jacked up on adrenaline, Sean stepped to the

shed doorway and let an arrow fly. But he was too amped up, and his fingers too numb with cold. He missed, the arrow flying over the heads of the two killers. But they were surprised and ducked defensively, without getting off a return gunshot.

Sinead had been blowing her steamy breath on her fingers, and stepped into the doorway, a hard, brittle glint in her blue eyes. Unconcerned about being fully exposed, she took careful aim, and let fly an arrow.

It hit Jake in the upper thigh.

The big man howled and reacted instinctively, breaking the arrow off and saying, "I'm hit, Anthony, I'm hit!" He winced with pain and gasped, "The lil shits shot me with a fookin arrow!"

Little Anthony fired off a quick shot to make the dangerous archers duck back into the shed. Then he assessed the damage to his brother. "You're bleedin, man ... but it doan look too deep. Here's my snot rag. Tie it tight round your leg. We need to get you off this mountain. Can ya walk?"

After pressing the handkerchief down hard for a few moments and then tying it against the broken-off arrow wound, Jake tried putting weight on his injured thigh. Painfully, he successfully shuffled forward a few steps and stopped. He gritted his teeth and mumbled, "Okay, it's bleedin and hurts big time, ya unnerstan. But maybe we can make it to the truck."

Little Anthony faced to the south, the old wagon trail covered with snow but visible in some windblown places. "Okay, the pickup isn't too far off in that direction. C'mon, man."

Jake limped along behind his brother, leaving a trail of crimson spots in the wake of his snowshoe prints.

## 12

Encouraged by the killers' sudden departure, Sean said with a grim edge of enthusiasm in his voice, "Let's follow them!"

"Yeah, after what they've done, we *can't* let them get away," Sinead said, her tone even more hard-edged than her brother's.

The two freshly invigorated archers were only fifty or so yards behind the fleeing killers, although they couldn't see them clearly because big snowflakes had begun to fall again, quickly covering up the men's snowshoe prints. But the wounded one left a trail, visible just under the layer of new-fallen snow … tiny scarlet flowers.

The twins waded through the snow, tracking their prey.

## 13

The Arthur brothers stopped to catch their breath, Little Anthony worriedly glancing back. He saw the telltale red spots disappearing back into the snowfall. "I think those two kids are probably stalking us, Jake. They're dangerous with those fucking bows."

The wounded brother glanced down and frowned at the red drops visible even under the new snow, and nodded.

"Can you make it to the pickup by yourself?" Little Anthony asked. He pointed up into a nearby thick cluster of low-growth madrone trees. "I'll hide up there and ambush their country asses."

Jake nodded, and then with a pained look of resignation on his features, he shuffled off along the trail southerly ... leaving larger, fresh bloody drops in his wake.

**14**

Even without snowshoes the twins were making good time, the new snowfall not too deep on this section of the windblown trail, which ran mostly along solid bedrock.

As they approached a section winding by a steep, forested slope ahead, they slowed and finally stopped. The luminescent apparition had appeared again, hovering over a nearby cluster of ghostly trees, just barely visible through the continuing snowfall.

Sinead said, "Our *friend* is signaling something to us, Sean."

He nodded, searching the ground sloping up to the trees, and finally spotted several snowshoe tracks not completely covered yet. He whispered back, "One of the killers is hiding up there in that madrone clump."

The strange hummingbird had delivered a third Christmas present to the twins.

"I'll drop back completely out of sight, and then circle around behind him. In five minutes you make some noise down here, and draw his full attention."

Sean came down slope behind the gunman, glancing toward the wagon trail, Sinead not visible through the heavy snowfall—

"Hey, Sean, catch up," his sister shouted.

The killer stood, lifted his automatic out front like a short dowsing rod, and moved slowly downhill to get a better shooting view.

Sean blew steamy breath onto his cold fingers for a moment, notched, and then let fly an arrow, hitting the man high in the middle of his upper back.

"*Ugh*," the killer grunted, but stayed upright, jerked around, and fired off a shot wildly.

Sean notched another arrow, aimed carefully, and shot the killer in the left side of his chest. A heart shot.

The man tumbled face down into the snow, just before Sinead appeared with a notched arrow ready in her bow. "You got him, Sean! Good!"

"Let's get the other wounded one," Sean said with fierce determination, leading his sister back down to the wagon trail, where they saw the bloodstains leading off south—

*Boom.*

The loud blast echoed around the startled teens.

Sean reached up to his left ear lobe, feeling as if he'd been stung by a wasp.

Looking back on the trail, about fifty feet away they saw the little man. He wasn't dead, but his face was dark scarlet with dried blood. He'd fired off a shotgun round, most of the pellets flying harmlessly over the twins' heads, but one stray had nicked the tip of Sean's ear lobe. The killer jacked another shell into the chamber of his sawed-off shotgun and sighted at the pair—

*Thunk.*

The small man suddenly straightened up and shuddered violently, his eyes wide and shocked … the tip of a sharp hunting arrowhead was poking out of his throat.

Just visible a few feet back on the trail was Uncle Mike, notching another hunting arrow. But the little man had tumbled forward face-first into the snow. And he wasn't moving.

Uncle Mike picked up the shotgun and hurried up to the twins. "I saw what happened to your folks up at the house. So sorry—"

He stopped as the words caught in his throat. He brushed at his eyes, sucked in a breath, and in a hoarser voice, said, "Then I tracked the snowshoe prints down to here.…" He paused to catch his breath. "You're hit," he added, finally noticing Sean's left ear.

Sean nodded, wiping blood from his ear lobe and said, "Not bad."

Sinead gently patted his wound with the tip of her blanket cloak. "I think it's okay," she said. "Let's get the last one, Uncle Mike. He's wounded and leaking blood big-time." She pointed south along the wagon trail.

"You okay to follow, Sean?" Uncle Mike asked.

Sean grinned wryly and said, "My ear's so numb from the cold, I can't feel a thing. Let's get him."

The three tracked the trail of snowshoe footprints and covered red flowers.

Finally, they spotted a Dodge Ram pickup parked ahead with a driver.

Cautiously, the twins spread out beyond either side of the trail, all three moving forward, alert for any aggressive movements.

Nothing.

They moved a few steps closer.

The wounded big man was slumped forward over the steering wheel … alive, but out cold. He'd apparently fainted from the loss of blood.

They disarmed the unconscious killer, tied his wrists together with plastic cuffs that they'd found in the big man's backpack.

The terrible Christmas nightmare had finally ended for the twins.

## EPILOGUE

*The translucent hummingbird appeared over a spot just north of the vacant horse shed. Then, it separated into hundreds of tiny dots, which hovered for a moment … then gently floated down to earth like luminescent greenish–blue snowflakes.*

# I SAW SANTA

## Steve Rasnic Tem

Tommy was eight years old when he first saw Santa in the flesh. Not some bloodless department-store Santa, but the real Santa who came through the chimney and ate whatever you left out there for him to eat and left whatever gifts he felt like leaving you.

Tommy had a habit of getting up most nights and wandering through the house. He was a little clumsy and was always running into things, always afraid his parents would hear him and lose their minds. That was a funny expression but he knew it was true. He'd seen them do exactly that—get so mad their faces changed until he didn't recognize them anymore and then they'd do things, stomp around and break his toys and hit him and stuff. Tommy was big for his age but he wasn't very strong. He got hurt easily. But at least he didn't complain about it. He kept his mouth shut when he got hurt.

Christmas Eve when Tommy was eight years old, he couldn't sleep. He lay in bed for a couple of hours just staring at the ceiling and listening to the house. They had an old house that made a lot of noise: pops and cracks and little stepping sounds like mice or cockroaches moving across the kitchen floor, or maybe even little men—who could know for sure? When his mom and dad were asleep and it was quiet enough he heard those little steps almost every night.

He got up that Christmas Eve and walked down the hall. He was really careful when he crept past his mom and dad's bedroom. He could hear them snoring—his mom sounding like she couldn't breathe, like someone was putting a hand over her mouth and then taking it away over and over again—she gasped like she was dying—his dad snarling and snorting like he was furious. Sometimes his dad talked in his sleep, and although Tommy couldn't understand the words he knew they were angry words.

His mom's fat black cat Mimi passed him in the hall. Mimi was his mom's cat because she was mean and scratched everybody else. His mom said it was because she was the only one who fed the damn thing and if some people would only do their share of the work then maybe that cat would like them too. Tommy tried to do his chores right but his mom said she might as well do them herself than let him screw things up again. Tommy didn't think the cat would like him even if he did feed her every once in awhile.

Tommy made it all the way downstairs to the living room without waking them up. He was proud of himself. Some day he would be the very best in the whole world at sneaking around. He just had to keep practicing.

Tommy pulled out his little red flashlight and let it shine on the floor and at the living room furniture and finally at the Christmas tree in the corner, dark now with its lights out. Tommy thought the tree was pretty special when they had the decorations on and everything all lit up. It didn't look that special now, though, all skinny and dark. Some of the ornaments lay scattered on the floor—Mimi liked to pull them off. He turned his flashlight off and on real fast a few times hoping that would make the tree special again but it didn't.

Tommy crept closer and shined his flashlight on the presents lying under the tree. There were new ones with his name on them, and they all said they were from Santa. But they were wrapped in the Christmas paper his mom had bought at the grocery store last week. He'd asked her about that before. She told him Santa might bring the presents, but she sure as hell had to wrap them.

Tommy could tell he didn't get anything he'd wanted. None of the packages were shaped like a football or a basketball or any other kind of ball. That was all he'd asked for. He'd learned not to ask for much, so that there would be less disappointment when he didn't get it. He picked up each wrapped package and shook it and was pretty sure they were all clothes. Well, he always needed clothes—he outgrew everything so fast. They were always telling him how much money he cost them. But he'd been hoping for something a little fun this year.

He heard a noise like a knock or a thump so he ducked behind the couch and put his ear against the floor. He figured he could hear someone coming from anywhere in the house that way. Then he heard steps across the floor, and then there was this thrumming inside his head like some kind of engine noise. He opened his eyes. It was Mimi, staring at him with her eyes wide. He waited for her to claw him but she didn't. Maybe she was in one of her rare good moods. Tommy put his head back down and closed his eyes, and eventually he went to sleep.

He woke up again and it was still dark, still the middle of the night. His ears were ringing like when he had a head cold, like someone was holding him underwater. He crawled on his hands and knees to the edge of the couch and looked around.

The Christmas tree lights were slowly blinking to life, a soft twinkling at first, then brighter and brighter, as if they were pulling in more and more electricity. A few of them became so bright Tommy was sure they were going to catch on fire.

The fireplace bricks began to shift and crumble. The floor was trembling. Tommy raised his hands, sure the bricks were going to fly across the room. Then something happened to the air, and he could feel this heavy pressure that stopped up his ears and made his face ache. A large red face suddenly appeared in the brick, like his dad's face when he'd been drinking too much. The face was pushing its way out of the brick, and then a red stocking cap appeared, popping out of the widening cracks, and there was Santa's bushy white beard moving around as if it were full of bugs. Then the rest of the body squeezed out of the bricks and Santa shook himself off. And when he shook he stank like a barn full of cows.

It was Santa all right, but looking nothing like any of the pictures Tommy had ever seen. Santa was taller than the Christmas tree and as wide as two refrigerators. His big, floppy face stretched out with a grin from one ear to the other. He yawned hugely and Tommy could smell his terrible breath and see his mouthful of rotting teeth. Santa's skin had gotten even redder, as red as a tomato. Tommy held his breath waiting for Santa's head to explode.

Santa looked around the room, frowning. "Where's my treat?" Tommy was afraid his mom and dad would hear and come downstairs. But maybe that was the least of his problems.

Then Santa stared right at Tommy. "Boy, come out of there! I *need* my treat! I've come a *long* way and I'm feeling a little light-headed."

Tommy crawled out from behind the couch and shakily stood up. "I guess there isn't one. I guess they didn't think you were coming."

"I see. Your mom and dad, *stingy* are they?"

"No, no. They're *nice* people, Santa. But they can't afford the moon, you know?"

"Is that what your daddy says, boy? Is he always talking about how he can't afford the moon, whatever you ask for? Well, I know the type."

His mom's cat walked between them. Santa looked down at it and grinned. "What's the cat's name, boy?"

"M-m-mimi, Sir."

"Mimi, hmmm. Sounds *yummy*."

"My mom keeps cookies hidden in a drawer!" Tommy said. "I'm not supposed to know, but I saw her put them there! I can get them for you—there's a whole bunch!"

"Well, don't just stand there! My tummy's growling!" Santa said. And it *was*. His belly sounded as if there were a bunch of angry dogs inside of it.

Tommy ran into the dining room and pulled three bags of cookies from underneath a folded tablecloth in one of the sideboard drawers. When he came back Santa swept them from his arms and stuffed them down his throat bags and all. Tommy could see a huge lump move down Santa's throat until it disappeared. "Got anything else?"

"Wasn't—wasn't that *enough*?"

Tommy started to back away, wondering if he could outrun Santa's long legs.

"Hmmm." Santa scratched his beard. A rat fell out of it and ran off into the dining room. Tommy could hear Mimi cry out as she began the chase. "Maybe so. I pretty much ate my fill at the Gibson house. You know the Gibsons?"

"I go to school with their son. Felix."

"Nice boy. *Very* nice. Well, maybe I've eaten enough for one night." He frowned at Tommy then, his eyes looking dark and ferocious. "You can't tell anyone about this, you hear? It's bad luck, catching Santa in the act."

Tommy nodded. "I won't, Santa."

"Good boy. Now good luck …" He scanned the floor with all its dust, ash, and rubble. "With all this." He turned toward the chimney.

"Bye, Santa," Tommy said.

"Wait!" Santa turned back around. "Almost forgot." He pounded himself on the chest a couple of times and opened his mouth, making a deep coughing sound.

Tommy stepped back. A glistening reddish-brown football flew out of Santa's mouth, which Tommy miraculously caught. It was soaking wet and slimy, a little stinky, but it appeared to be brand new.

Santa wiped the drool off his mouth and said, "You might want to hide that, by the way, to avoid any embarrassing questions." He backed into the fireplace and started to fade into it. "Next year, don't be afraid to ask for more. As long as you remember them treats." And then he was gone.

Tommy started to sweep up some of the dust but of course there was no way he could fix all the broken bricks around the fireplace so he finally gave up and just went to bed. The next morning he woke up to the sounds of his dad yelling and cursing and stomping around. He went downstairs to face whatever his parents wanted to do to him.

"I know you did this—I just don't know how you did this," his dad said quietly, staring at him. When Tommy's dad used his soft voice like that he was even scarier. Tommy wondered if he ran out the door right then if his dad could catch him. The old man was drinking already, so maybe not.

"That boy couldn't break those bricks—he's not strong enough. You've seen him try to lift things—he's useless." His mom patted his dad's arm as she said this. Of course she wasn't defending Tommy—she just didn't want his dad to go on a rampage and *completely* ruin the holiday.

That all changed later that day when she discovered that the cookies were missing. Tommy went to bed without Christmas dinner, with a promise that next year he was getting nothing at all. Of course he knew his parents wouldn't remember that long, and underneath his bed he still had that bright and shiny new football.

For Christmas of his ninth year Tommy asked for a chemistry set. His mom and dad looked at him as if he were crazy. "There's no way!" his dad said.

"But if *Santa* brings it, can I keep it?"

His mom and dad looked at each other. His mother shrugged. His dad smiled grimly. "Sure, kid. If Santa is stupid enough to bring you something you'll blow yourself up with, sure, you can keep the damn thing."

Late Christmas Eve Tommy snuck down to the living room with a giant bag of goodies he'd been hoarding for months: licorice sticks and candy corn and apples and oranges and stale Easter Peeps, a giant bag of candy saved from Halloween, and two full jars of peanut butter and jam.

Mimi, older, still fat and still annoying kept trying to grab the treats and he had to push her away with his foot. Once she dug her claws deep into his knee and he had to bite his lip to keep from screaming. He spent some time arranging the treats in front of the fireplace (completely repaired by his dad, although several of the bricks were a different shade of red and had been put in crookedly) so that Santa would see them as soon as he appeared.

Tommy was almost finished when he felt that ringing in his ears, and then a pressure so strong it made him drop to the floor. He closed his eyes against the pain and several hard and heavy things fell on his back. He started crawling on his hands and knees as fast as he could to get away.

He bumped into something cool and smooth and he opened his eyes. It was massive, black, and shiny. Tommy leaned back a little. It was a giant boot. Looking up he saw the colossal swollen head nodding toward him, the burning black eyes and lively beard, the cheeks glowing purple. Santa grinned a shark's grin—his teeth were several inches long and came down to needle-like points.

"You're bigger," Santa said. "Too many burgers? Or is it ice cream?" Tom scrambled to his feet and backed away. Santa was so wide he hid the fireplace from view, but when he bent down and began gobbling up his treats Tommy could see that the fireplace was almost completely destroyed. One of Santa's boots crushed part of the Christmas tree, which hadn't been all that big in the first place.

Santa's oversized head wobbled like one of those carnival bobble heads as he looked around the room. "You still have that football I gave you last year?"

"Y-yes," Tommy replied. "I only play with it with my friends at the playground. M-mom and Dad, they still don't know I h-have it."

"Oh, *you* have friends?" Santa puffed out his huge blubbery lips like he didn't believe him.

"That's mean, Santa."

"Just kidding!" Santa boomed. "Don't be so *serious!*" He laughed, his belly moving in massive waves that knocked half of the living room furniture over. Tommy was glad his mom and dad had been drinking so heavily that night. Still, he wondered what might happen if they woke up and saw Santa like this. The idea of seeing their terrified faces thrilled him. "But is this *all* the treats you have? I'm *starving!* Can't you see how I'm *wasting* away?"

That stupid cat Mimi walked between them then, and before Tommy could say anything else Santa stretched out an enormous black-gloved hand and scooped the cat up and dropped her into his gaping mouth. Santa chewed some, grinding his teeth so loudly it drowned out the cat's screeches, and then he pounded his chest hard as he swallowed.

Tommy started to cry, wondering if Santa was going to eat him next.

"Hush, boy. Are you saying you *liked* that cat? Tell the truth—I know you didn't!" Tommy shook his head. "No—that's what I thought. I'm satisfied now, thanks for asking. I just needed a little protein, you know? Protein builds muscle. You need more protein, boy!"

Tommy nodded dumbly. How was he going to explain the missing cat? He looked around at the devastation. How was he going to explain any of this?

Santa put a finger to his nose with a drunken-looking lop-sided grin. After a minute or two with nothing happening he sighed and shook his head. Then he turned and disappeared into the gigantic hole where the fireplace used to be.

Tommy woke up the next morning to a lot of rage and anger, but much to his surprise none of it was directed at him. He came downstairs to see his dad screaming on the phone at someone from the insurance company. More of the wall behind the fireplace had collapsed, leaving a clear view to the outside. He could see his mom through the hole, out in the yard calling for Mimi. Dust and bricks were everywhere. Whatever was left of the Christmas tree lay on its side, covered in rubble.

"I don't know *when* it happened! We were *asleep*, dammit! How should *I* know? It's been a rough holiday—we needed our sleep, I guess. I *work* for a living! I just want you to do your *job* and get out here!" His dad slammed down the phone. He looked at Tommy, frowning. "Somebody drove into the side of the house last night. You didn't hear anything?"

Tommy shook his head. "Not a peep."

"Well, neither did we. And that damn *cat* ran away."

His mother came stumbling back inside through the hole in the wall. Tommy thought to tell her how dangerous that was, but figured he'd better keep his mouth shut. Her face was wet from crying, which surprised him. He never thought she might actually love that cat. "Well, she's gone for good!" she cried. "Or else they took her."

"Who the hell would want …" his father began, but then the terrible look on his mom's face stopped all conversation.

It wasn't until they were cleaning up that afternoon that his dad found the package in the corner, undamaged. "What the hell is *this!*" He held up a giant brightly-colored box. *Junior Mad Scientist's Chemistry Set!* was emblazoned in neon green lettering across the front of the box.

"It looks like Santa brought me that chemistry set I asked for," Tommy said, beaming.

His dad glanced at the kitchen where his mother was fixing dinner. "I'll kill her," he muttered.

"You *said* I could keep it if *Santa* brought it," Tommy said, not quite able to get rid of his smile.

His dad put down the box and went upstairs for the rest of the day.

Tommy spent most of the next year gathering together everything he could think of that a monstrous and unpredictable Santa might eat. His parents never came into his room anymore, so he had no worries about them finding anything.

Some of these Santa treats were canned goods he'd pilfered from the kitchen, taken one can at a time and not very often so his mother didn't suspect anything. Now and then he'd take one of his dad's beers, and once a bottle of whiskey hidden in some towels. That caused a big fight between his mom and dad, but they were always fighting anyway, so he didn't feel too guilty about it. They were still fighting over who gave him that chemistry set—each calling the other a liar.

By the time his tenth Christmas rolled around Tommy had ample food to feed an army of regular Santas, and he hoped it would somehow satisfy this monster Santa once and for all. He had a dozen or more boxes of canned food, huge stacks of stale bread loaves, sacks full of candies and spoiled fruit, and a load of stuff no normal person would eat—rotten fish heads and a dead squirrel and his old marble collection.

His dad lost his job early in the year and was home most of the time drinking. His mom worked long hours for a house-cleaning company and was so tired and disgusted when she got home she didn't clean their own house anymore. Most nights they had pizza or Tommy heated up his own ramen noodle soup.

He didn't know how his dad survived—Tommy hardly ever saw him eat.

But he made a long Christmas list anyway. What did it matter? Santa was the one who brought the good presents. Tommy asked for a big kid's bike, video game console, a weight lifting set, skateboard, a box of toy soldiers, a bunch of adventure books, and so many other things he couldn't remember them all. His parents took one look at his list and didn't say a word. Later he found it crumpled up in the trash.

On Christmas Eve his parents went to bed early, leaving Tommy by himself. They never got around to decorating the tree, so Tommy made ornaments out of construction paper, tape and glue, and hung them from the sparse branches.

It took a long time to haul all of Santa's food downstairs. At least there weren't any presents around taking up space. If his parents had bought him anything, he certainly hadn't seen evidence of it.

The fireplace had been rebuilt with the insurance money. The investigator couldn't understand why there were no tire tracks out in the yard, but couldn't come up with any other rational explanation for the damage. The company paid, and then canceled their home insurance. His dad had railed about it all year long.

Tommy didn't know what they'd do if the fireplace was destroyed again. Maybe they'd have to move. Not such a bad thing—maybe Santa wouldn't be able to find them at a new address.

As soon as the last bit of food was in place Tommy felt a rumbling deep beneath his feet, then the house began to shake, mildly at first but increasing until pictures were falling off the walls. He felt a sudden blast of heat behind him and turned around to discover a fire in the new fireplace.

He studied the flames. They came to multiple points like a mouthful of glowing red teeth. Then he noticed the huge deep-set eyes at the back of the fireplace.

The interior of the fireplace was pushing out towards him, expanding, becoming this fierce red face, dragging flaming whiskers and hair and sideburns behind it, and an elongated body that might have been a giant snake's, but which Tommy now realized looked more like a train.

It poured its way down the chimney and out of the fireplace and across the living room.

A double door slid open in the side of the train and a naked red elf appeared, throwing a shiny new bicycle out into the room. Tommy grabbed it and immediately climbed on. It was incredible. He drove it into the dining room and rode it around the table a few times as the Santa train roared through the living room consuming everything in sight—not only the food, but the tree and all the furniture disappearing into its flaming maw. "Ho ho ho!" tooted the Santa horn.

Tommy stopped and looked into Santa's train engine face. "Is this all I get?"

The Santa train roared, flames shooting out of its mouth. "Is that all *you get?* What else do you have to *feed* me?"

Tommy thought for a second. "Well I guess there's some food in the refrigerator. Leftovers mostly, my mom doesn't…"

Before he could finish the Santa train was locomoting into the kitchen, narrowing itself to get through the door. There was an explosive racket of metal screeches and heavy things being pushed around, cabinets scraped from walls and their contents crashing to the hard linoleum floor.

All this made Tommy very nervous, so he rode his new bike around the table a few more times. It was all he could think of to do.

"Tommy?" It was his mother's voice. He looked back into the living room, and his parents were standing there in their pajamas and robes. It surprised him how colorless they looked. Compared to everything else they looked like they had no color at all. They were like black-and-white people who had accidentally wandered into a color movie.

Tommy rode his bike around the table as fast as he could. "See what Santa brought me? Santa brought me a new bike!"

The Santa train came roaring out of the kitchen with its mouth, whiskers and eyebrows on fire. It opened its fiery maw and swallowed Tommy's mom and dad whole. They screamed for a moment, but their screams were replaced by the Santa train's roars of delight.

"So what *else* do you want?" the Santa train bellowed.

"I can't decide I can't decide!" Tommy cried, still racing his bike around the table.

The train door slid open again and three naked red elves waved. They were surrounded by countless shelves overflowing with what appeared to be toys, but it was hard to tell exactly what they were, or how far the shelves extended. Just the glimpse made Tommy's mouth go dry with excitement. "Then come inside come inside!" the elves cried in unison.

And after once more around the table, that's exactly what Tommy did, the door snapping shut so quickly behind him it severed his bike in two.

# DECEMBER BIRTHDAY

## Jeff Strand

### 10 YEARS AGO

"It's a birthday present *and* a Christmas present!" said Aunt Jenny, as Clyde opened the box and looked at his new pair of gloves.

"Thanks," said Clyde.

### 9 YEARS AGO

"Happy birthday!" said Grandma over the phone. "You excited about Christmas? Santa Claus is almost here! I hope you were good!"

"I was," said Clyde.

### 8 YEARS AGO

"It's a birthday present *and* Christmas present!" said Jake. "My mom said it was okay to do it that way and you were probably used to it."

"That's fine," said Clyde.

### 7 YEARS AGO

"I can't come to your party," said Melissa. "All my relatives are in town. We're putting up the tree tonight."

"Okay," said Clyde.

### 6 YEARS AGO

"Your birthday present's in Christmas paper because it's both a birthday *and* a Christmas present," said Amy.

"How thoughtful," said Clyde.

### 5 YEARS AGO

"You're lucky, Clyde," said Mortimer. "I never get to go out caroling on my birthday!"

"It's great," said Clyde.

# December Birthday

## ▲ YEARS AGO

"Happy birthday!" said Abigail. "Here's your present! You can't open it until the 25th, though. It's a birthday *and* a Christmas present!"

"That makes sense," said Clyde.

## 3 YEARS AGO

"Oh, I'd love to go," said Henry, "but I don't know when we're going to get back from the mall. I haven't started my Christmas shopping."

"No problem," said Clyde.

## 2 YEARS AGO

"Thank you," said Clyde. "I didn't even know they made a Christmas edition of Monopoly."

"Since it's a birthday *and* a Christmas present, I wanted to get you something appropriate," said Joe.

"Of course," said Clyde.

## 1 YEAR AGO

"Sorry it's just a card," said Daphne. "I'm broke

around the holidays. You know how it is."

"Yes," said Clyde.

**TODAY**

"It's a birthday present *and* a Christmas present," said Uncle Mitch.

"Thank you," said Clyde, just before he reached under his Christmas sweater, took out a revolver, and shot Uncle Mitch in the face. Blood and brain matter splattered against the tree.

Everybody screamed.

"Who else wants to give me a combination birthday/Christmas present?" Clyde demanded, waving the gun around at the other five people in the living room. "Anybody? C'mon, I know you motherfuckers have more combined gifts for me! *Who else?*"

"Just calm down," said Dad, stepping forward. "There's no reason to get upset."

Clyde pointed the gun at their elderly next door neighbor. "Hey, Mrs. Grayson! You brought over a gift, didn't you? I see it right there on the dining room table! Nice red and green paper! I love the candy cane under the bow—very festive! How about you go get my present so we can continue the celebration, huh?"

"I don't think this is the appropriate time," said Mrs. Grayson.

"I disagree! It's party time, bitch! Go get it!"

Trembling and weeping, the old woman stood up and slowly walked into the dining room. She suddenly turned and tried to make a run for it, but her left foot twisted underneath her and she fell to the floor.

Clyde stormed into the dining room. He picked the package up by the ribbon. "Oh, look. It's to Clyde. Happy Birthday/Merry Christmas."

"I'm sorry!" said Mrs. Grayson. "Money is tight during the holi—"

Clyde threw the present to the floor, then shot her in the throat.

He waved the gun at the remaining four people. "Nobody move! My present to myself is that I get to watch her die!"

Mrs. Grayson clutched at her neck, blood spurting between her fingers. She was dead before "God Rest Ye Merry Gentlemen" had finished playing on the radio.

"Who's next?" Clyde asked.

"Please calm down," said Dad. "Please, son, you have to remember that the true spirit of Christmas is about giving, not receiving!"

"Fuck you, Dad!" Clyde shouted, shooting Dad in the stomach. "That bullet was for Christmas *and* your birthday! How does it feel? How does it feel, Dad?"

"We never did that!" Dad insisted, as he fell to the floor. Mom let out a wail of anguish and horror.

"No, but you let it happen! You didn't protect me from the others! Betty always had a huge July celebration! She had clowns and ponies at her parties! Where were my clowns and ponies, Dad? *Where were my clowns and ponies?*"

"We're sorry!" said Mom. "It wasn't our fault! You were unplanned! We never would have done this to you on purpose! We'd just moved into our own home and we weren't used to having privacy!"

"You ruined my life!"

Mom gestured around the living room. "But, sweetheart, we're having a party for you right now!"

"Bullshit! This isn't a birthday party! These

people happened to stop over!" He shot Aunt Penny between the eyes. Before she'd finished tumbling out of the recliner, he pointed the gun at the postman. "He's just here because you offered him hot cocoa!"

"There are a bunch of birthday presents for you out in my truck!" said the postman. "I was going to get them after I finished my cocoa! I'll go right out and get them!"

Clyde shot the postman in the head. He spilled the hot drink all over his lap but was too dead to feel the scalding pain.

"Please, son …" said Dad. "Don't … don't do this …" He coughed up some blood, then began to sing. *"Happy birthday … to … you … happy … birth … day ……… to …"* His eyes glazed over and he went silent.

*"… you …"* Mom continued. *"Happy Birthday dear Clyde, happy—"*

Clyde shot her.

"I totally get where you're coming from," said the last person alive, Mr. Taylor, who lived two houses down. "My birthday isn't just in December. My birthday is on *Christmas.*"

"That must suck," said Clyde.

"Oh, God, does it ever! One year my parents

just put candles in the fruitcake. Can you imagine? So I understand what you're going through. I understand why you wanted to go on a killing spree. But I am not your enemy. I'm the only one who truly knows your anguish."

"Let me see your driver's license," said Clyde.

"What?"

"I said, let me see your driver's license or some other form of identification."

"I, uh, didn't bring my wallet with me."

"What's your zodiac sign?"

"Huh? Oh, uh…"

"You lying piece of crap," said Clyde, before he pulled the trigger. Mr. Taylor's nose exploded.

Clyde gazed at the corpses. Some would call it an extreme reaction. Some would dismiss him as a lunatic. But he'd share his message with all who would listen.

He could hear sirens in the distance. Clyde went into the kitchen, where his birthday cake rested on the counter. He lit the candles and took a deep breath.

He could be the catalyst of change for

future generations. He could be a cautionary tale of the dangers of downplaying birthdays just because of their proximity to the most popular holiday of the year.

Clyde made his birthday wish and blew out the candles.

# A NOTE FROM SANTA

*William F. Nolan*

Do you believe in ghosts? Well, *I* sure do. With good reason. I *met* one, a real nasty one. I'd just gone down the chimney of this home in Kansas City. Old part of town. Rundown. But I had to stop off and deliver some toys to this little ten-year-old brat, which I did. Left 'em by the big Christmas tree in the living room. The kid was still asleep.

And that's when this ghost showed up, fierce-looking. A mean SOB, that's for sure. Lemme tell you, not all ghosts are vapory. This one was solid. Came at me with an axe!

Swung it at me. I ducked under the blade and lit out for the chimney. Climbed back to the roof. Looked down. There he was, peering up the chimney at me and shaking his axe.

Well, as I was watching him, he just began misting away, till there was nothing left of him but his axe. Oh, he was a ghost all right. No doubt of that.

I was lucky to be alive!

And that's why I believe in ghosts.

# SILENT NIGHT

*Richard Chizmar*

The man sat in his car parked alongside the cemetery and finished his cigarette. The engine was off and the driver's window was down. It was raining, not too hard, not too soft, a steady rain that drummed the man a lonely lullaby on the roof of his car and soaked his left elbow, which was propped out the window.

He reached over with a gloved hand and dropped the butt into an empty water bottle sitting on the passenger seat next to him. He did this by feel, never once taking his eyes off the cemetery grounds. He scanned from left to right, and back again.

The cemetery had been crowded earlier—always was this time of year—but now the grounds were nearly abandoned thanks to the late hour and the cold and rain. His eyes touched an elderly man a few hundred yards to his right. The old man had been there for the better part of an hour, standing still and rigid, staring down at a grave marker, lost in thought and memory. A middle-aged couple knelt on the wet ground directly in front of the man's car, maybe a hundred yards out. Had they lost a child, the man wondered? Or were they mourning a mother or father or both? The man thought it could have been all three. The way this world works.

The old-timer left first, weaving his way surprisingly fast between the headstones to a faded red pickup. The truck started with a backfire that sounded too much like a gunshot and slunk away into the twilight. The man watched the taillights fade to tiny red sparks and imagined a dinner table set for one awaiting the old man at home.

Five minutes later, the middle-aged man helped the middle-aged woman to her feet, and with wet knees they walked hand-in-hand to a gray SUV parked at the opposite end of the road. The middle-aged woman never looked up, but the middle-aged man did. Just before he opened his car door and got inside, he glanced back at the man and nodded.

The man remained perfectly still in his car. He didn't return the nod and he didn't lift a hand to wave. He cast his eyes downward for a moment out of habit, an old trick, but he knew it wasn't necessary. He was being paranoid again. He gauged the distance at sixty yards and it was raining and his wipers weren't on. The middle-aged man was merely nodding at a dark shape behind blurry glass; a polite acknowledgement that he and the man sitting alone in his car both belonged to the same somber fraternity. A moment of kindness shared, and nothing else.

The man watched the middle-aged couple drive away and fought the urge to light up another cigarette. He scanned the cemetery grounds, left to right and back again, waited five more minutes to be sure, and then he got out of the car.

In Forest Hills Memorial Gardens at 6:19 p.m. on December 24th a single man exits the lone car that remains parked on cemetery property, a dark sedan with rental license plates. The man is of medium height but broad in his chest and shoulders. He looks around, like he's making sure he's alone, straightens his jacket, lowers his winter hat, and despite walking with a slight limp, he makes his way quickly and confidently to a nearby gravesite. The man's eyes never stop moving beneath that winter hat, and the path he takes is precise and direct. The man has been here before.

Once he reaches his destination, the man bends down and places a single red rose at the base of a headstone, where it joins several other much fancier flower arrangements and a plastic Santa decoration with a candle inside, its flame long since drenched by the falling December rain. The man traces a finger along the names engraved on the marker. He is wearing gloves on both of his hands, and there's a flash of dark gunmetal at the back of the man's waistband.

The man doesn't linger. He quickly stands up, readjusts his jacket and once again surveys the cemetery, slower this time, as if he somehow senses a presence there in the trees, and then he heads back to his car without a backward glance.

Within a heartbeat of closing his car door, the man starts the engine and speeds out of the cemetery. Headlights off and nary a tapping of brake lights. A dark shadow swallowed by the night and the approaching storm.

High in the towering pines, the rain changes over to snow and the wind picks up, whispering its secrets. But the cemetery is deserted now and there is no one left to hear.

"Are you Santa Claus?"

The man stopped in mid-step, one foot in the kitchen, one foot still in the family room, staring over his shoulder at the little boy standing in the glow of the Christmas tree lights. The boy was wearing red-and-white pajamas and blinking sleep from his eyes. The man slowly removed his hand from the gun in his waistband, where it had instinctually moved to at the sound of the boy's voice, turned around, and lifted a finger to his lips. *Sshhh*.

The little boy—nine years old and named Peter, the man knew—wrinkled his nose in confusion, but stayed quiet.

The man slowly stepped back into the family room. His hands held out in front of him. "It's okay," he whispered. "I was just on my way out."

The little boy moved closer, unafraid, and

whispered right back, "If you're not Santa, then who are you?"

The man didn't know what to say, so he just stood there, memorizing every inch of the little boy. He had entered the house twenty minutes earlier through the basement door. It had been too easy; he hadn't even needed to use his special tools. He'd crept up the carpeted stairs, silent as a housecat, and eased his way into a dark kitchen, and then the family room, where he'd found a Christmas tree tucked into the corner by the fireplace with dozens of wrapped presents waiting beneath it. The man had stood there in the quiet darkness for a long time, taking it all in. The decorations on the tree, many of which he recognized. The framed pictures on the mantle, several featuring the man's younger, smiling face. He stared at the paintings on the wall, the knickknacks on the shelves, the furniture, even the curtains. This was the man's first—and most likely last—time inside the new house, and he wanted to soak up everything he could into his memory banks … to remember later.

Somehow he had missed the little boy, who'd probably snuck downstairs after his mother had fallen asleep and curled up on the sofa beneath a blanket waiting for Santa. Some agent he was.

"You know what? You look a lot like my Uncle Bobby," the little boy whispered, his cute little nose all wrinkled up again. "Only his hair is a lot longer than yours."

The man felt his eyes grow wet and fought it back. His pulse quickened. There was so much he wanted to say. So much he needed to say.

But he knew he couldn't.

The letter and box of money he had placed under the tree would have to be enough.

The man reached out and rested a shaky, gloved hand on the boy's small shoulder.

"Give your mom and Uncle Bobby a hug for me. I bet they're awesome folks." The man bent down and kissed the top of the boy's head— and that was when he smelled her on the little boy. His wife. Even after all those years.

Inhaling deeply, voice shaking now, the man said, "I left you all something under the tree."

The little boy's eyes flashed wide and, with a smile, he looked back at the Christmas tree. "What did you leave us?" he asked.

But when he turned back around, the man was gone.

✳

Even with the drifting snow and occasional tears blurring his vision, the man traveled back roads to the airport, careful to make certain no one was following him. He hoped he was just being paranoid, but he couldn't be sure. It had been a quiet fifteen months since they had almost found him in Mexico. Two years before that, they had somehow tracked him to the coast of Venezuela, and it was only with God's good grace that he'd remained a free man. They would never stop looking, and he would never stop running. He knew too much; had seen and done too much.

The plows hadn't touched most of the back roads, so the going was slow. That was okay with the man. The airport was only twenty-seven miles away, and he had almost three hours to return the rental car and make his gate for the return flight overseas. Better safe than sorry, he thought, although even if a policeman found him stuck on the side of the road in a ditch, he should be fine. His rental papers were in order, and he carried a legal driver's license, credit cards, Social Security card and everything else he needed to appear a normal, law-abiding U.S. citizen. If, for any reason, the cop decided to search his rental car, then that would be another story. The man would be forced to resort to other options.

With that thought in mind, the man glanced in the rearview mirror and dropped his speed another five miles per hour. He turned the windshield wipers up a notch. The man knew he would have to be at his most vigilant at the airport. These days, they watched the international flights with special attention, especially around the holidays. He would dispose of his weapons once he reached the rental-car return lot, but not a moment sooner.

Ten minutes later, the winding back road he was traveling on merged with MD Route 40 and soon after he passed an old-fashioned road sign that read: WELCOME TO EDGEWOOD. The man looked at the sign with a sad smile.

Maybe a mile later, he slowed through an intersection beneath a blinking yellow traffic light that was dancing wildly in the whipping wind and snow. There was a strip mall bordering the right side of the road, all the stores gone dark except for a Dunkin' Donuts at the far end of the building. Twin mounds of snow covered two small cars in the parking lot, probably belonging to the unfortunate workers inside.

The man tapped the brakes and steered into the parking lot, feeling his back tires slide a little in the accumulating slush. He swung around and parked facing the road, away from the Dunkin' Donuts front windows, and turned off the car. His eyes had grown weary, and he knew from experience that strong coffee was the remedy. His stomach was talking to him, too. He thought maybe a couple chocolate donuts or a hot breakfast sandwich, if they served those this time of night.

The man got out of his car and watched as a snowplow loomed out of the darkness like some kind of huge prehistoric animal, its glowing yellow eyes illuminating the swirling snow. The driver flipped him a wave from inside the warmth of his cab, and this time the man waved back. He was halfway to the front door of Dunkin' Donuts when his wrist began to vibrate. Startled, the man looked down at his arm and thumbed a button on the side of his watch, silencing it.

It was midnight.

*Christmas.*

The man stopped in the middle of the parking lot, oblivious to the cold and falling snow. It had been ten Christmases since he'd last held her in his arms. Ten impossibly long years. She had been pregnant with his child then—with Peter. They had been so excited that they were going to be parents. They had painted and decorated the nursery together. Shopped for outfits and baby supplies. They had been happy.

Six months later, on a routine assignment in Turkey, the man had found himself in the wrong place at the wrong time—and instead of helping him, his government had tried to solve the problem by erasing his existence. He'd been on the run ever since. Running from dangerous men trained just as he had been trained, from men he once called his brothers. They would laugh at him now, the man thought. Tired and hungry and crying, sneaking back home like a scared mouse in the forest. They had taught him better than that. They had taught him to be superhuman. Invisible. Immortal.

The man let out a deep breath and watched the vapor fill the air in front of his face. The night was hushed and serene, not even the falling snow hitting the store's front windows making a sound, and it made the man think of nights like this when he'd been just a kid, sledding down Hanson Hill long after dark with his neighborhood friends, their excited voices echoing across the snowy fields.

The man glanced down Route 40 toward the blinking yellow traffic light. Imagined driving back there and turning left, cruising two miles up Hanson Road to the house he had grown up in. It had been a happy house. Filled with board games and books and laughter. Filled with the love of his parents and his baby brother and the eternal mysteries of three older sisters.

Then he imagined turning left at the intersection, taking Mountain Road until it spilled into 22, following it for twenty minutes or so until it took him right back to the cemetery.

The cemetery …

… where his mother and father had been buried.

… where the United States Government had claimed to bury him with full military honors.

The man stood there alone in the middle of the strip mall parking lot, his hands beginning to shake despite his gloves, his mind betraying him with visions of empty coffins buried in frozen ground and little boys looking up at him with wide, innocent eyes, asking, *"Are you Santa Claus?"*

And this time he couldn't stop the tears from falling. Sloppy cold tears, equal parts shame and regret.

He should have answered him, the man thought in a panic. He should have told him, "That's right, son, I'm Santa. My red suit's in the wash ..."

Or at the very least—the truth. He owed him that much. "No, not Santa, son. I'm no one. Just a ghost."

Instead, he'd said nothing and snuck away into the night.

Out on the road, another snowplow roared by, heading in the opposite direction.

The man blinked, as if waking from a deep dream, turned around and walked back to his car. He got inside and drove away.

Away from the only home he'd ever known.

Away from everything.

*"A ghost,"* the man whispered to himself in the darkness and drove on toward the airport.

The man wasn't tired or hungry anymore.

Edited by Chris Morey
Interior design by Michael Bailey
Individual works © 2017 by individual authors

Dark Regions Press, LLC
P.O. Box 31022
Portland, OR 97231
United States of America
DarkRegions.com

First Trade Paperback Edition
ISBN: 978-1-62641-276-7

eBook
ISBN: 978-1-62641-277-4

Made in the USA
San Bernardino, CA
26 December 2017